E FICTION INK

Inkpen, Deborah.

Harriet and the Little Fat
Fairy

03
7113

For my parents

my children

my husband

and two hamsters

FICTION
INK

First edition for the United States and the Philippines
published 2002 by Barron's Educational Series, Inc.

Published by arrangement with Hodder Children's Books

First published in 2002 by Hodder Children's Books

All inquiries should be addressed to:
Barron's Educational Series, Inc.
250 Wireless Boulevard
Hauppauge, New York 11788
http://www.barronseduc.com

Library of Congress Catalog Card No.: 2001099618

International Standard Book No.: 0-7641-5562-8

PRINTED IN HONG KONG
9 8 7 6 5 4 3 2 1

HARRIET
AND THE LITTLE FAT FAIRY

DEBORAH INKPEN

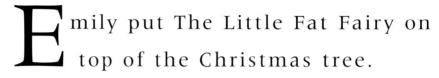

Emily put The Little Fat Fairy on
top of the Christmas tree.

"Now, don't fall off again!" she said.

The fairy smiled blankly.

Emily jumped down from the

chair and ran to Harriet's

cage.

She lifted the little

hamster gently from

her nest.

"It's Christmas Eve,"

she whispered.

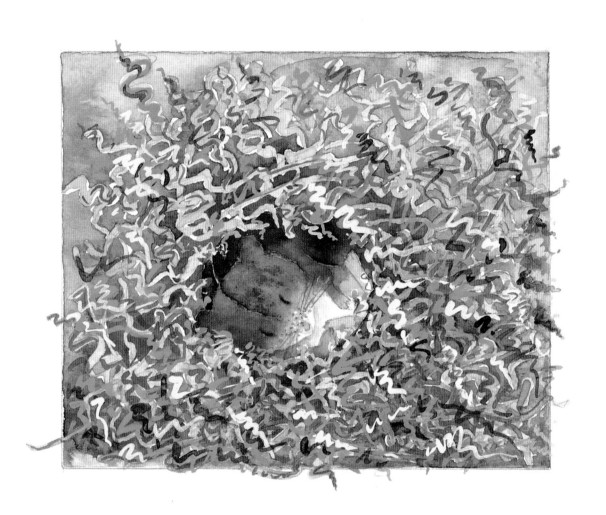

Emily took her over to the Christmas tree.

"Look," she said, stretching out her hand.

Harriet opened one eye. A huge, dark, spiky shape towered above her. It was covered in hundreds of fairy lights that seemed to dance and twinkle all around her.

Harriet sniffed the air. It smelled of pine trees.

S he crawled to the end of Emily's hand. The pine needles prickled her nose.

She stretched a little further, lost her balance, and fell, landing upside down on one of the branches.

E mily giggled. "You don't make a
very good Christmas decoration,"
she said. She took some tinsel and
popped it on Harriet's head.

"That's better," said Emily.

H arriet's tinsel floated to the floor.
Emily caught it. When she looked up,
Harriet had gone.

"Oh, no!" cried Emily.

She peered into the branches. She could
just make out Harriet's little pink nose.
She dived under the tree, searching
desperately through the maze of prickly
branches and Christmas decorations.

Harriet had disappeared.

At the top of the tree
The Little Fat Fairy
continued to smile.

Harriet began to explore her sparkly, new world. She peered into a shiny, gold bauble. A funny little face peered back.

S he tried nibbling a red
plastic berry.
It was hard and tasteless.

Then she nibbled a
chocolate snowman.
That tasted better, once
she had chewed past the
silver paper.

Emily's brother Billy came to help.

They caught glimpses of Harriet, scampering through the branches but always just out of reach.

After a while they lost sight of her altogether. They sat down, their hands scratched and sore.

"She's probably left the tree by now," said Billy. "She could be anywhere!" Emily looked tearful.

"Let's put her cage under the Christmas tree," he said. "Perhaps she will find her own way home."

Emily wrote a letter to Santa Claus.
"Dear Santa, please can you bring back
my hamster?"

Emily's mom warned her daughter, as
she grabbed her hat and coat, that
Santa Claus very busy on Christmas
Eve, and perhaps he would not
have time to answer her letter.

Emily said she was sure
he would. But her mother didn't
hear. She had already left to
go shopping.

Emily thought for a moment and
then added,

"P.S. And could you bring her a friend?"

Harriet had not left the Christmas tree.
She was busily climbing through the branches
and had come across some very curious things.

A tiny straw reindeer,

a tin Santa Claus,

A painted, cardboard teddy bear,

and a little red basket,
which fit her perfectly.

Emily and Billy spent the afternoon drawing until their mom returned from shopping. She was carrying a little white box, which she took upstairs, before joining them for a snack.

"Harriet's not back yet?" she asked. They shook their heads.

Emily had one last look under the tree before bedtime.

The cage was still empty.

"Don't worry," said her mom, as she tucked
Emily into bed. "I expect she will turn up."
When she was sure that Emily and Billy were
fast asleep, Emily's mom picked up the box and
tiptoed downstairs to the Christmas tree.

At the top of the Christmas tree Harriet came face to face with The Little Fat Fairy. As she scrambled up onto the fairy's shoulder, the slender branch began to wobble.

They balanced there for a moment, then the fairy toppled forward. She tumbled down through the branches, taking Harriet with her.

H
arriet landed with a thud on top of the fairy.

She rolled on to the floor. . .

. . .and sat up next to her cage. Curled up inside was a Russian hamster, just like herself!

Harriet lay still for a moment, just watching, wondering what to do. She tried the cage door. It was shut tight. She ran up and down the bars. There was no way in.

The Little Fat Fairy lay nearby. Exhausted from her adventure, Harriet nuzzled into the fairy's soft, shimmery dress.

As she closed her eyes she heard the sound of sleigh bells. By the time Santa Claus arrived, Harriet was fast asleep.

When Emily came down on Christmas morning, Harriet was back in her cage, and she was not alone!

"Wow!" said Billy.

"Oh, my goodness!" said Mom. "Three hamsters!"

"Santa Claus did answer my letter!" said Emily. "I knew he would!"

As she bent down to open the cage, Emily spotted the fairy.

"Fallen off again?" she said. The Little Fat Fairy just smiled back.